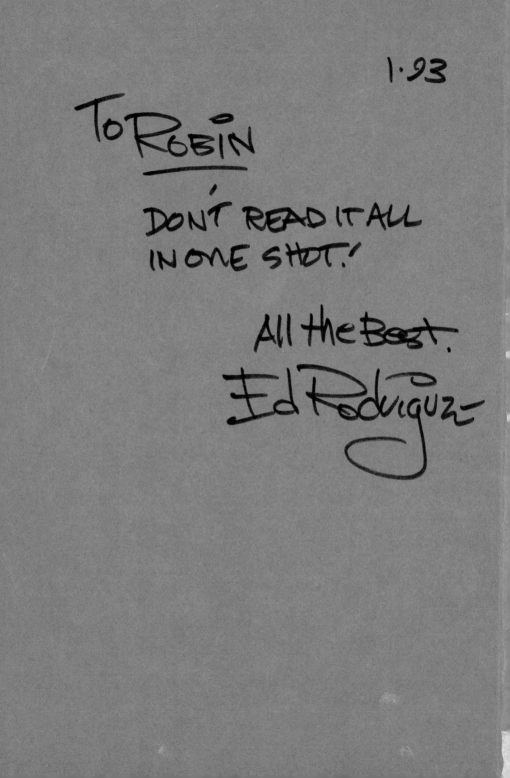

THE ART CLASS

By Gina Ingoglia

Illustrated by
Ed Rodriguez

DISNEP
PRESS

NEW YORK

FIRST EDITION

1   3   5   7   9   10   8   6   4   2

Library of Congress Catalog Card Number: 91-58786
ISBN: 1-56282-047-8 / 1-56282-227-6 (lib. bdg.)

Donald ran up the steps.

He was late for school.

Art class had started.

"Hi," said Donald. "Here I am!"

"Hi, Donald," said Minnie and Daisy.

Mickey and Goofy waved to him.

"What are you doing?"
Donald asked Minnie.
"I am drawing a picture
of Goofy," said Minnie.
"I am drawing a line
around him."

Donald picked up a crayon.

"I will help you," he said.

"I will show you how

I make a line!"

Minnie said, "Donald!
That is wrong.
You are making
a wavy line!"

"I like wavy lines,"
Donald said.
"Some of my favorite animals
are wavy.
Worms are wavy.
Snakes and eels
are wavy, too."

Minnie took the crayon
from Donald.

"Look at what you did!"
she said.

"Now I have to start over!
Go away, Donald," said Minnie.

"What are you doing?"
Donald asked Daisy.
"I am painting a picture
for a window," said Daisy.
"I am painting
red and blue dots."

"I will help you,"
said Donald.
He picked up a brush.
It had red paint on it.
Donald put the brush
into the blue paint.

"Look at what happened!"

said Donald.

"I mixed the red paint

with the blue paint.

It turned purple!

Now you can make purple dots."

"I do not want purple dots,"
said Daisy.

"Why not?" asked Donald.

"Some of my favorite foods
are purple.

I like to eat purple grapes.

I love grape jam.

Purple lollipops are very good, too."

Daisy said, "I do not care!
Go away, Donald."

"Hi, Mickey," said Donald.

"What are you doing?"

"I am cutting out shapes,"
said Mickey.

"I am making a mobile."

Donald looked at the shapes.

"You need some circles," he said.

"I do not want circles,"
said Mickey.

"Yes, you do," said Donald.

He cut out a circle for Mickey.

"Some of my favorite things

are circles," Donald said.

"The sun is a great big circle.

Cookies are circles.

And so are pennies

and dimes

and nickels

and quarters."

Mickey put his hands
over his ears.
"Stop!" he shouted.
"I do not want circles!
Go away!" Mickey said.

"All right," said Donald.

"I will work by myself."

He found some paint

and a brush.

He found some paste

and paper.

Then Donald began to work.

Donald said, "I will make
lots of purple paint!"
He mixed some red paint
with some blue paint.
"It is easy to make
new colors," said Donald.
"Mixing colors is fun!"

Donald took out some paper.

He painted the paper purple.

"This looks good,"

he said.

Next Donald cut out circles.

He cut out big circles.

He cut out little circles.

He cut out red circles.

He cut out blue circles.

He cut out green circles.

He cut out yellow circles.

Donald pasted the circles

on the purple paper.

29

Donald stepped back.

He looked at his work.

"It needs wavy lines," he said.

He pasted wavy yarn

on his picture.

"I like this!"

Donald said.

"Look at what I did,"

said Donald.

Everybody came to see.

"I like purple," said Donald.

"I like circles.

I like wavy lines.

I put them all together!"

Art class was over.

Donald looked around the room.

"We are all good artists,"

he said.

"Do you know what I really like?"
he asked.

"What?" asked Minnie.

"Art class!" he shouted.

ART NOTES

Shapes

Squares ☐

Rectangles ▭

Triangles △

Circles ○

Colors

Red, yellow, and blue
are called basic colors.
You can mix them together
to make other colors.
Red and yellow make orange.
Red and blue make purple.
Yellow and blue make green.

Lines

Lines can be

Straight

Wavy

Dotted

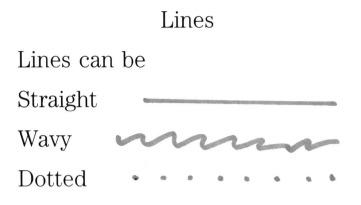

Minnie and Goofy's Real-life Pictures

What you need:

A friend

Crayons

Construction paper

(big enough to lie on top of)

Put the construction paper

on the floor.

Have your friend
lie on the paper.
Draw a black
crayon line around
your friend.
Make sure to draw
fingers and shoes.

Now it is your turn.
Lie on a new piece of paper.
Have your friend
draw a line around you.

Draw faces and clothes
on your outline.
Now you have life-size pictures—
just as big as you are!

Daisy's Window Paintings

What you need:

Paper napkins

Water

Watercolor paints or
small bottles of vegetable colors
Paintbrushes
Newspaper to protect the table

Spread newspaper
on the table.
Paint designs on
a folded napkin.

The paints will spread
and run together.
Make sure the paint
goes through all the layers
of the napkin.
Let the napkin dry!

Unfold the napkin.

You will see a beautiful design.

Tape the napkin to a window.

The colors glow

in the sunlight.

You have a bright window picture!

Here are some designs

you might try.

But it is fun to make

your own pretty window pictures.

Mickey's Mobile

What you need:

Wire clothes hanger

Construction paper

(at least two different colors)

Paste

Scissors

Yarn

Cut some yarn into short pieces.

Cut some yarn into long pieces.

Tie the yarn to the hanger.

Draw shapes on red paper.

Make any shapes you like.

Cut them out.

Put the red shapes

on yellow paper.

Draw an outline around them.

Cut out the yellow shapes.

Now you have the same shapes

in red and yellow.

(You can use any colors you like.)

Paste the red shapes on the yarn.

Paste the yellow shapes on top
of the same red shapes.
The yarn is pasted
between each shape.

Now you have a mobile!
Hang it in a doorway
or near a window.
The wind makes the shapes turn
and look pretty.

Donald's Collage

What you need:

Paste

Scissors

Cardboard

Paste paper and other objects
on a large piece
of cardboard.

You can use many things
to make a great collage,
including the following:

Stamps

Uncooked pasta

Dried beans

Pictures from magazines

47

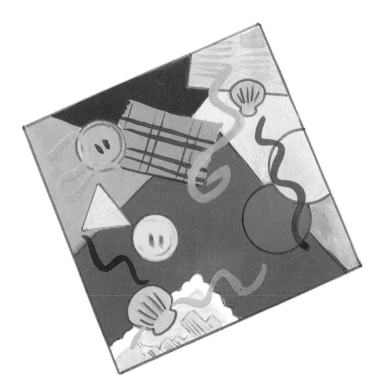

Newspaper clippings

Postcards

Colored paper

Bits of cloth

Small seashells

Buttons

Labels from cans

Yarn